THE BOXCAR CHILDREN®

CREATED BY
GERTRUDE CHANDLER WARNER

INTERACTIVE MYSTERY

THE GREAT SPY SHOWDOWN

STORY BY **JM LEE**

ILLUSTRATED BY **HOLLIE HIBBERT**

ALBERT WHITMAN & COMPANY
CHICAGO, ILLINOIS

First published in the United States of America
in 2019 by Albert Whitman & Company

ISBN 978-0-8075-2860-0 (paperback)
ISBN 978-0-8075-2861-7 (ebook)

Printed in the United States of America
10 9 8 7 6 5 4 3 2 1 LB 24 23 22 21 20 19

Illustrations by Hollie Hibbert

Visit the Boxcar Children online at www.boxcarchildren.com.
For more information about Albert Whitman & Company,
visit our website at www.albertwhitman.com.

100 years of Albert Whitman & Company
Celebrate with us in 2019!

THE GREAT SPY SHOWDOWN

INTERACTIVE MYSTERY

CHOOSE A PATH.
FOLLOW THE CLUES.
SOLVE THE MYSTERY!

Can you help the Boxcar Children crack the case? Follow the directions at the end of each section to decide what the Aldens do next. But beware—some routes will end the story before the case is solved. After you finish one path, go back and follow the other paths to see how it all turns out!

INVITATION

"I'll be at the coffee shop across the street. Come over when you're all set!" said Grandfather. The Aldens were in front of a bookshop in downtown Greenfield. It was a bright and sunny winter day, just cold enough that their breath fogged in the air.

"And don't rush," Grandfather added. "Any time spent in a bookshop is time well spent!"

"You got it," said fourteen-year-old Henry, the oldest of the Alden children. "We'll find you when we're done."

"And *you* don't drink too much coffee!" said Jessie. At twelve, Jessie was younger than Henry, but she was often looking after her siblings—and sometimes Grandfather.

"I won't!" Grandfather said. With a chuckle,

he tipped his cap and waved, heading across the street to the café.

Violet's cheeks were getting pink from the chilly air. She rubbed her nose with her soft, fluffy mitten and eagerly opened the door to the bookshop. There was no ten-year-old who loved reading more than Violet. "I can't wait to look around," she said, hurrying inside.

"When we're done, maybe we can join Grandfather and get some hot cocoa!" said Benny, the last one inside. At six, he was the youngest Alden, and he was usually thinking about snacks. But as soon as he looked inside the bookstore, he forgot all about hot cocoa.

It was a small shop, but every wall was covered end-to-end with books. And in the center of the room were even more rows, each marked with a sign. Benny sounded out the words on the signs. "Mystery," he said, using a quiet voice. "Fiction. Nonfiction...oh! Those are the types of books on those shelves."

"That's right," said Henry. "The books are sorted by genre."

"Genre?" Benny did not know that word. "Is that like the type of book?"

Henry nodded. "Exactly. Fantasy, science fiction, history—those are categories books fall into. It's easier to find books if they are organized that way."

"Jessie, can we get a new Agent Ada book?" Benny asked.

"Sure," said Jessie. "I heard the new one just came out last week. Let's see if you can find it yourself. What *genre* do you think it would be?"

Benny folded his arms and tapped his chin like he'd seen Henry do when he was thinking. "Let's see. Agent Ada is a spy. She's fifteen years old. Is there a type of book for teenage spies?"

Jessie smiled. "I don't think this shop has a whole shelf for books about teenage spies."

"There is a children's and young adult section though," said Violet. "I bet we can find Agent Ada over there."

The Aldens wove through the maze of shelves until they got to the back corner of the shop. There, two bookshelves were filled with the types of books Benny recognized. Some were books for people just learning to read, like him. Others, like the Agent Ada series, were bigger books with chapters in them. Benny wasn't ready to read those yet, but he loved it when Jessie and Henry read them aloud to him and Violet.

"All right, Agent Ada," Jessie said, putting her hands on her hips. "Where are you?"

Violet brought Benny closer to the bookshelf. "See, Benny? Once you find the right genre, the books are organized by the author's last name."

"Agent Ada books are by A.D. Ashton," Benny said, scanning the names of the authors. "I remember because A.D. Ashton sounds like Ada—it's a funny coincidence."

"I don't think it's a coincidence," said Henry. "I think A.D. Ashton is a pen name. That's when an author puts a made-up name on their books."

"Why would the author do that?" asked Benny, looking up at Henry.

"Hmm..." said Henry. "I suppose I don't know. But I'm sure he has his reasons. Some people just like to keep their lives private, you know? Using a pen name protects his identity."

The Great Spy Showdown

Benny nodded and started looking for the Agent Ada books again. "I guess that makes sense. Like Agent Ada always says, 'A spy should never reveal another spy's secret identity!' But if I wrote a book, I'd want everyone to know I was the author."

Violet stood on a little footstool to reach the top shelf on the left. She skimmed the spines, reading the titles and author names quietly. *Adams, Anderson, Archer...* "Here it is, Benny! I found the Agent Ada books."

Violet took a book from the shelf and hopped off the footstool. She handed it to Benny, and his eyes widened with excitement. On the cover was Agent Ada, the main character of the series. She had black hair in a ponytail and wore her signature black scarf wrapped high around her face, so only her eyes showed.

"*Agent Ada and the Techno Caper,*" Violet said, reading the title.

"That's the new one!" Benny said. "Let's skip the hot cocoa and go home and read the whole thing!"

Henry laughed. "Take it easy. If we read it all at once, it'll be over too fast."

"Henry's right," Violet said. "Let's take our time and make it last."

"Oh, fine," Benny said. "Violet, let's see what else is here. Maybe there are other books about spies that we might like too."

As the Aldens split up, Jessie found her way to the gardening section. She wanted to find the perfect flowers to plant by the boxcar for when spring came around.

At one time, Henry, Jessie, Violet, and Benny had lived in the boxcar. That was after their parents had died. It was the only place the children could find. It wasn't much, but they had been together as a family, and they had come to love it. So when Grandfather found them and brought them to live in Greenfield, he had brought the boxcar too. Now it sat in their backyard, and they used it as their clubhouse.

"It would look lovely with daffodils," Jessie said to herself, imagining light-yellow flowers beside the red boxcar.

All of a sudden, Jessie felt a tickling on her shoulder. It felt as though someone was watching

her. Jessie looked around but didn't see anyone. Maybe I imagined it, she thought to herself.

After a while, the Aldens gathered at the register. Benny and Violet had each found a second book they wanted to read, and Henry had two thick sports books. Jessie added her book about perennials to the pile, making six books altogether.

The clerk was an older woman with thick gray hair and even thicker glasses, which made her eyes look big and round like an owl's. She smiled as she rang up the books, putting them one at a time into a paper bag. After she was done, she reached to hand Henry the change.

"Oops!" Four coins slipped out of the clerk's hand. Henry, Jessie, Violet, and Benny all stooped to pick the coins up off the ground.

When Jessie stood back up, she saw the clerk smoothing out the paper bag. "Sorry about that," the clerk said. It almost seemed as if her big owl eyes were smiling, but it was difficult to tell through her glasses. "My fingers aren't as nimble as they used to be."

"It's no problem, ma'am," said Henry. The Aldens

thanked the clerk and left the store, bundling up and hurrying across the street to the café.

They found Grandfather enjoying a mug of tea while he read the paper. "Did you find some bookish treasures?" he asked.

"Yes, we each found something we liked," Violet said.

"And we got the newest Agent Ada book to read together," said Benny, showing Grandfather.

"*Techno-Caper*, eh?" asked Grandfather, raising a brow. "Sounds very exciting. That Ada always uses interesting gadgets during her adventures. Sounds like this one will be extra exciting...Oh, what's this?"

A slip of paper was sticking out of the Agent Ada book. Violet took it out from between the pages. It looked like a bookmark made out of fancy silver paper with black ink.

Violet read the writing on the bookmark and gasped.

"What does it say?" Benny asked.

"It's an invitation," said Violet. She gave the bookmark to Henry, who read it aloud.

The Great Spy Showdown

Dear Young Ada-mirers,

You are cordially invited to the Great Spy Showdown, a competition to put your sleuthing and spy skills to the test. Four teams have been chosen, but only one will win the chance to meet A.D. Ashton, author of the Agent Ada spy series.

"A spy competition?" Jessie said with a gasp of delight. "And only four teams are invited—we got pretty lucky, didn't we?"

"Grandfather, can we go?" Violet asked. "After all of our mysteries and adventures, we've learned a lot about getting information. I bet we could win and meet A.D. Ashton—maybe even learn his real name!"

Grandfather looked over the bookmark. "Looks like the competition is happening upstate, in Chester Hills—very nice area and a lovely drive as well. Of course you can go. I would be glad to take you."

"Hooray!" cried Benny.

The Great Spy Showdown

While Benny and Violet finished their cocoa, Jessie turned the bookmark over and back again.

"I don't remember seeing this in the Agent Ada book when we brought it to the checkout counter," she said to Henry.

"Me either," said Henry. "That's strange, but it would have been easy to miss."

Jessie slipped the bookmark back into the book with a smile. Perhaps the excitement of the spy competition had already begun.

CONTINUE TO PAGE 12

ARRIVAL

On the day of the Great Spy Showdown, Henry, Jessie, Violet, and Benny climbed into Grandfather's car and rode through the snow-covered hills to the address written on the invitation. Their destination was a large estate in a grove of dark green trees, sitting atop a hill that overlooked rolling valleys filled with soft white snow.

The manor itself was large and modern. There was a main entryway with an identical-looking wing on either side. The lantern near the front door was decorated with ribbons that were the same color as the bookmark the Aldens had received.

A big chalkboard sign in the driveway read: *Welcome Agents!*

"Looks like we found the right place," Grandfather

said. He parked the car, and the five of them got out, looking over the hills and valleys sparkling with fresh snow. It had taken most of the afternoon to arrive, and the sun was just starting to set.

"Those hills look perfect for skiing," said Jessie. She was a good skier, though it had been a while since she'd been on a slope as steep as the ones they were looking at. Most of the time, she helped Violet learn on the bunny hill in Greenfield.

"They certainly are," Grandfather said, his warm breath puffing in clouds. "Those hills and mountains are full of ski resorts. This is a very popular area for winter sports. I used to come out here to ski all the time when I was a young man. Boy, it gets dark out fast in the winter, doesn't it?"

"*Bonsoir!*"

An older man in a black tuxedo was waiting for them on the path to the manor. The man had a thick gray mustache and a large mole over his right eyebrow.

"Hello, hello. You must be the Aldens," he said with a heavy French accent. "I am Benedict, A.D. Ashton's butler. You must be James Alden, the

children's grandfather. So good to meet you. Will you be staying in the manor? The competition is scheduled for the entire weekend."

"Oh, no, thank you," Grandfather said. He winked at the children. "You know those ski resorts I visited as a lad? Well, the truth is, I booked myself a room at one. While you are exercising your sleuthing skills, I'll be enjoying a hot mug of coffee and gazing out over the beautiful vista. Good luck in the competition. I'll see you afterward!"

Grandfather tipped his hat and waved good-bye.

"Very well. Let us go inside where it is warm," Benedict said, and he led the Aldens inside to a reception hall, where he gave a bow. "Now then! Allow me to welcome you to the Great Spy Showdown."

It may have only been the entryway, but it was quite grand. The floor tiles were white, and the woodwork in the trim and along the staircase were dark brown. A large glass case showed off dozens of golden awards and medals, surrounded by framed diplomas and certificates. But the most impressive thing in the room was an eye-catching portrait of a woman, which hung on the wall across from the door. She wore a fancy, peach-colored dress and held up a pair of opera binoculars, hiding her eyes. Her lips had a slight smile, as if she was keeping a secret.

Violet gasped. "This looks just like the manor that Agent Ada lives in with her uncle. It's like we've walked right into the Agent Ada books."

"I wonder if there are trapdoors and hidden rooms here too!" said Benny.

"That would be quite mysterious, *non*?" said Benedict. Then he cleared his throat. "Welcome to the Ashton Manor, where A.D. Ashton, the author of the Agent Ada series, lives and does all of the writing."

"All twenty-eight books?" Violet asked.

"All twenty-eight," Benedict said with a proud nod. "Now...let me explain the competition. There will be three rounds, each focusing on skills any successful spy should have. In each round, one team will be eliminated. And as you saw in the invitation, the last team standing will be awarded the opportunity to meet A.D. Ashton."

"And we're staying here in the manor?" Jessie asked.

"Indeed. Your rooms have been prepared. However, right now we have some preparations to make for the competition. As you know, it is vital for a spy to make the most of the technology at their disposal. Accordingly, using technology will be an important part of this competition. Two of you will now report to the Gadgetry, where you will be trained on the equipment you will be using. The other two will come with me for a brief tour of your living quarters. There you will leave your things and find the rest of the gear for the competition. Afterward, we will all proceed to dinner before retiring for the evening. The competition begins first thing tomorrow morning."

Henry nodded toward the sounds of voices from down the hall. "Have the other teams arrived already?" he asked.

"*Oui*," Benedict said with a nod. "There are four teams in all, and each has been designated a number. You four are Team One. Each team is made of four agents ages six to sixteen. Benny, you are the youngest, but do not fear. Agent Ada was also very young when she first began her spy training."

Benny stood up a little straighter. He liked the idea of getting a head start on his spy training.

"Are the other teams brothers and sisters like us?" asked Violet.

"*Non*. You are the only team that is siblings," said Benedict. "And you are the final team to arrive. And so, time is of the essence. Your first decision must now be made: Who will be going to the Gadgetry, and who will be going on the tour?"

"I'd like to see the Gadgetry," Violet said.

"And I want to see the rest of the manor," Benny said. He took Jessie's hand. "And maybe find something to eat..."

Jessie chuckled. "I guess you're going with Violet then, Henry."

"Great," Henry said. "All right, Aldens, missions are confirmed. Let's split up."

The Great Spy Showdown

TO FOLLOW HENRY AND VIOLET TO THE GADGETRY,
GO TO PAGE 20.

TO FOLLOW JESSIE AND BENNY ON THE TOUR,
GO TO PAGE 31.

The Gadgetry

"Very well," Benedict said. "Henry and Violet, head down this hall to the Gadgetry. It is at the end of the west wing and will be difficult to miss. Dr. Sharpe will be introducing the technology very soon."

Violet and Henry went where Benedict indicated. As they walked, they noticed more certificates and diplomas hanging in neat rows. Although Violet didn't have time to stop and look closely, she did notice something strange.

"There aren't any names on these certificates," she said. "I think A.D. Ashton must really want to keep his identity a secret."

Henry glanced at one of the certificates. It was an award for Electronic Lock Picking. Henry had seen Grandfather's university diploma hanging in his office. On it, Grandfather's name, James Henry Alden, was written clearly at the bottom. But A.D. Ashton's certificates and diplomas were very different. On the line where a name might go, there was only a blank line and the word *Agent*.

"Maybe that's how they do it in spy school," said Henry.

"Agent Ada always says a spy's most important tool is their identity," Violet said. She shivered. "How mysterious!"

At the end of the hall was a set of doors that opened to a large room with a high ceiling. The room reminded Henry of the science lab at school, with four worktables in two rows. At the far end, a brown desk sat in front of tall windows overlooking the surrounding hills.

The voices quieted when Henry and Violet entered. Two members from each of the other three teams were already there. Each pair stood at their own worktable, where they had opened a metal briefcase to reveal a collection of gadgets. Each table also had a sign with a team number on it. Everyone hushed to watch Henry and Violet find their place at the Team One worktable.

At first, Violet wasn't sure how to react to the other teams. They were the competition, after all. But just as she and Henry took their seats, one of the children from the table next to theirs waved and gave a friendly smile. Violet let out a breath and waved back. After a moment, the quiet conversations in the room started up again.

"The gadgets must be inside the cases," Violet said. "I can't wait to see what's inside. My favorite Agent Ada gadgets are invisible ink and those nano-hook gloves she uses to climb walls like a gecko."

"I hope we get to use a grappling hook," Henry said. "Let's open it up!"

Henry flipped open the case. The inside was padded with black foam to protect the equipment inside. Henry and Violet took all the gadgets out carefully and laid them side by side on the table.

The first item was a computer tablet. It was about the size of the notebook Jessie used to keep lists. Violet set it beside two headsets, which each came with a small watch to control the settings. Henry took out the biggest gadget in the case, which looked sort of like a toy helicopter Violet had seen at the store.

"What is that?" Violet asked.

"It's a drone," Henry said, setting it down gently. The drone was made of black plastic and had four arms, each with a little propeller. In the center was a glass lens that Violet realized was a camera. Henry showed her the controller, which was small, with two joysticks and a few buttons. "We can control it with this. I bet the camera in the center feeds into the tablet."

"So cool!" Violet said quietly. "Jessie's going to love the tablet for taking notes, and Benny's going to have a lot of fun playing with the drone."

"Remember, this isn't all about fun," Henry said. "These are expensive pieces of equipment. We'll also have to be careful with them. Hey, I think I see something else in the case. What's that?"

Henry was right. Violet looked and found one final gadget resting in the case. But when she set it on the table, it didn't look nearly as high-tech as the rest of the gadgets. It was just a pair of regular sunglasses.

"Hmm," Henry said as they looked them over.

"I bet there's something special about them. Let's wait for Dr. Sharpe, who I'm sure will explain."

As if on cue, a shrill voice rang out as a tall woman came into the room, carrying yet another metal case. "Good evening, agents!" She seemed even taller thanks to a high-tech-looking helmet with a ridge that stuck up on the top. The woman stood in front of the desk and introduced herself.

"I am Dr. Elizabeth Sharpe, A.D. Ashton's technology consultant. Whenever A.D. Ashton writes a new book that involves technology, I help make sure the description is accurate. I'm also a professor of experimental engineering. I was asked to come in today to train you all on the gadgets you'll be using for the competition. Please follow along as I review the equipment."

Dr. Sharpe set her case on the desk and opened it. One at a time, she removed the items and explained.

"This is a tablet, also called an electronic notebook. You can use it to take notes and photographs. Remember that documenting your observations is an important part of being a good spy. The tablet is also linked with the drone, and the video captured by the drone's camera will automatically show up on the tablet, so you can view it."

Next she took out the drone. She set it on the desk and turned it on using the controller. The lights blinked, the propellers spun, and after a moment, it gently lifted into the air, gliding smoothly in a figure eight overhead.

"These drones are controlled with the handset. Use the two joysticks to control direction and height. To turn on the camera, use the button in the center. You may find the drones useful for looking at things you couldn't otherwise see. Remember, Agent Ada always says, 'If you're ever stuck, try looking at things from a different angle.'"

The third thing Dr. Sharpe went over were the headsets. "The headsets can be tuned to two channels—one open channel that is shared between all of the headsets. Use that one in case of any emergencies. The second channel is a private channel, which is only shared between the two headsets in your team. And lastly"—Dr. Sharpe held up the glasses—"I won't say much about these except to tell you that they will prove invaluable. Someone on your team should be wearing them at all times. Now! Take a moment to familiarize yourself with your gadgets. I'll come around and answer any questions you may have."

The room burst into conversation as the teams started experimenting with the equipment. Violet put on one of the headsets and turned on the tablet while Henry powered up the drone. A moment later, Violet saw the video feed from the drone's camera appear on the tablet.

"Here we go," Henry said. He pushed forward on one of the joysticks, and the drone started to hover. But as soon as Henry touched the other joystick, the drone began to jerk and wobble. Henry chewed on his lip, eyes focused.

"This is a lot harder than Dr. Sharpe made it look," he said.

"Wow, look at Team Three's drone," Violet said, nodding with her chin.

Although Team Two and Team Four were having the same challenge as Henry, Team Three's drone was swooping through the room quickly and smoothly. The boy controlling it was about her age, ten or eleven, Violet guessed. The boy watched the drone with a little smile.

"Looks like Team Three has a real techno whiz," Henry said, arching his eyebrow. He concentrated on their own drone, eyes sparkling with determination. "I'll really have to practice now!"

While Henry worked on flying the drone, Violet turned her attention to the headset. Using the watch, she found that the headset had two settings, 0 and 1. She pressed the first one and listened.

"Once we win, we'll have to make sure to get a photo with A.D. Ashton."

Violet looked around the room. Someone was broadcasting on the open frequency. Team Three was distracted watching the drone, and Team Four was trying on the glasses. It was the two members from Team Two that were using the headsets.

"Yes, we'll have to get a photo if we want our plan to work," said the older of the pair, a boy about Henry's age. He was whispering, but Violet could hear him because he was wearing the headset.

Violet turned off her headset and took it off.

"Henry, I just heard something strange," she said quietly. "The members of Team Two are talking about getting a photo of A.D. Ashton and some kind of plan. I think they were talking about it on the open frequency by accident...I don't know what they meant, but it didn't sound very nice."

"Hmm, that does sound strange," said Henry. "Let's keep an eye on Team Two."

A little later, Dr. Sharpe returned to the front of the room.

"Good work today, agents," she said. "Now, unless anyone has any other questions, you're free to bring your equipment up to your rooms and join the others for dinner. Tomorrow your first mission will begin."

The four teams packed their gadgets into the cases. As they all got ready to leave, Dr. Sharpe cleared her throat.

"Oh, one more thing that I almost forgot. The winning team gets to keep the gadgets they used for the competition," she said. The children gasped with excitement. Even Violet couldn't help but imagine what fun she and her siblings could have with the drone and the tablet and the headsets— even the mysterious glasses. Dr. Sharpe winked and waved them off.

"Very good, now hurry along," she said. "And good luck to you all!"

CONTINUE TO PAGE 41

THE TOUR

Benedict gave Henry and Violet directions to the Gadgetry, then turned back to Jessie and Benny. With an elegant gesture, he waved them toward the staircase at the back of the entryway.

"This way, please!" he said.

The manor was large, though not as big as some of the historic mansions Jessie and her siblings had visited. She and Benny followed Benedict up to the second floor, then down a hallway with plush gray carpet.

"The manor has two main wings," Benedict explained as they walked. "This is the west wing. On the first floor is the kitchen, the dining hall, and the Gadgetry. On the second floor is where each team's suite is located. You are welcome to explore the manor during the day, but we ask that you do not enter the east wing. That is A.D. Ashton's private living space, and out of respect, please do not venture there unless requested."

"Understood!" Jessie said.

Benny nodded and repeated, "Understood!"

At the end of the hall was an open room with a fireplace, sofas, and a television. Despite being in such a fancy manor, the room was cozy, almost like the family room at Grandfather's house.

"This common area is for the four teams to share during the competition. You can think of it as your home base," Benedict explained. Surrounding the common area were four doors, each with a sign saying what team they were for. When Benedict reached the first door, he unlocked it and handed Jessie the key.

"This will be your room for the duration of the competition," he said, opening the door and waving them inside. "There are four beds and a private shower. I hope you will find everything satisfactory."

"Thank you so much," Jessie said. "I'm sure it will be."

The Great Spy Showdown

Benedict bowed. "Now then, I must go and prepare supper. Please make yourselves at home, and when you are ready, join us in the dining hall." Then he turned and left them to take in their room.

It was like Benedict had said: a medium-size room with four beds, a dresser, and a big window overlooking the snowy hills outside. Jessie set their luggage down in the closet and took off her coat.

"This home base is really nice!" Benny said. "Wow, cool! Check this out!"

On one of the beds sat four sets of black clothing. The outfits were each made up of a pair of black pants with many pockets, a simple black T-shirt, a black utility belt, and a sharp-looking black jacket. Even though the jacket wasn't as bulky as Jessie's winter coat, she could tell from the thick lining that it would be plenty warm.

"These are so cool!" Benny said. He tried on the smallest jacket. It fit perfectly. "Do I look as cool as Ada?" he asked with a big smile.

"I don't know if anyone can look as cool as Ada," Jessie said, teasing him. She slipped on her own jacket. It fit just right too. She wanted to try on the utility belt—the whole outfit, really—but they'd have plenty of time for that later. She took off the jacket and put it back on the bed. She saw an envelope lying next to the black spy outfits. It said *TEAM 1* on the front.

"What's it say?" said Benny.

Inside the envelope was a note and four blank place cards. Jessie read the note: "'All good spies use code names to protect their secret identities. All competitors will use code names for the competition. Once you have picked code names for your team, join the other teams in the dining hall for supper.'"

"Code names?" Benny asked. "I've always wanted a code name! I want to be...Boxcar Benny!"

Jessie laughed. "Benny, you can't have your real name in your code name. It's supposed to *hide* your identity, not tell everyone who you are. It should be a cool way for other people to describe you, kind of like a superhero name."

"Hmm..." Benny thought hard. "Well, you are supersmart. And you like to write things down.

I think you should be Professor J. The J stands for Jessie."

Jessie smiled. "Thank you, Benny. I will be Professor J. What do you want to be?

Benny thought hard again. "Hot Dog."

"Hot Dog and Professor J, huh?" Jessie said with a smile. She found a marker in her backpack and wrote *Hot Dog* and *Professor J* on two of the cards. "How about Henry and Violet?"

"Hmm. Violet is a color," Benny said. "What's another word for *violet*? Purple?"

"How about *amethyst*?" Jessie said. "She could be Agent Amethyst."

Benny lit up with excitement. "I like that! And Henry should be Cluemaster. He's always using clues to solve hard puzzles."

Jessie wrote the code names on the place cards. "Cluemaster, Professor J, Amethyst, and Hot Dog," she said. "We sound like quite the spy team. Now we're all set for dinner."

The two closed up their room and followed Benedict's directions to the dining hall. When they got close, Benny sniffed the air. Jessie did too.

"Do I smell tomato soup?" Jessie asked.

"Jessie!" Benny said, grabbing Jessie's hand. "Tomato soup and avocado toast is Agent Ada's favorite. Do you think that's what we're having?"

Jessie laughed. "How perfect. *And* we get to eat supper in A.D. Ashton's dining hall...I don't think I can be disappointed, even if we don't win the competition."

The dining hall was a wide room with another big fireplace and a long table. Slices of golden toast topped with avocado spread were arranged on a white platter, and a large kettle of soup was warming over an electric heater. It looked just like the pictures of Agent Ada's suppers.

Jessie and Benny took their seats and set out their name cards, leaving two empty chairs for Henry and Violet. Some of the other team members were there too, two from each team. Jessie guessed everyone else was still in the Gadgetry, where Henry and Violet were.

"I can't wait to eat. This looks so good," Benny said, holding his stomach. "I guess we should wait until everyone is here though."

The Great Spy Showdown

"Hello," said the girl sitting across the table from Jessie. She was from Team Three, according to her place card. She looked like she was about Henry's age, and she wore a pretty blue hijab wrapped around her hair and face. "I'm—well, my code name is InfraRed. Nice to meet you!"

"Hello, I'm..." Jessie remembered to use her code name when introducing herself. "I'm Professor J. Dinner smells delicious, doesn't it?"

"Yes, I can't wait," InfraRed said warmly.

"Can you believe it?" said one of the boys from Team Four. His place card said *Scott*. He had fluffy brown hair and was smiling from ear to ear. "We are going to eat Ada's favorite food in A.D. Ashton's house!"

A tall, older boy with dark hair near the head of the table, a member of Team Two, snorted and crossed his arms. His place card said *Chameleon*. He sat next to a girl whose code name was *Leopard*. She had her blond hair pulled into a bun. Neither of them was smiling.

"Calm down," Chameleon said. "This is a competition. But you might not have noticed that part yet, since you didn't even write down a code name, *Scott*."

Scott's ears turned red. He looked down at his shoes.

"That's not very nice," Jessie said to Chameleon. "This weekend is going to be fun, even if we don't win."

Leopard laughed, but it wasn't very nice sounding.

"I'm glad you think that, since you're definitely not going to win," she said. "After all, you've got a *baby* on your team."

"Hey, I'm six!" Benny said.

InfraRed spoke up. "Come on, Leopard. There's no reason to be mean like that." She faced Chameleon and Leopard. Her partner, a younger boy who was just about Benny's age, nodded. His code name was Gigabyte.

"Yeah. You've been nothing but mean to everyone since you got here," Gigabyte said. "If you're not going to be a good sport, you might as well leave everyone alone."

Chameleon snorted again and turned away. Leopard rolled her eyes but said nothing.

"Just ignore them," Jessie told Benny.

"You're right," said Benny. "I'm not going to let him ruin my avocado toast and tomato soup."

After a little while, the other members of the teams arrived. Jessie thought everyone seemed friendly enough, except for the members of Team Two, who quietly whispered among themselves.

Once everyone was seated, Benedict came in and removed the lid from the kettle.

"Dinner is served," he said. The scent of the soup made Jessie's mouth water. Moments later, everyone had a piece of avocado toast and a bowl of steaming tomato soup. The bread was crisp and buttery, and the soup was just a little spicy. Jessie had never tasted a better combination.

"Do you think A.D. Ashton is going to join us?" Benny asked between mouthfuls of toast.

"I don't know," Jessie said. "Come to think of it, the only adult we've seen so far is Benedict."

"A.D. Ashton is very secretive," said Scott. Another member of his team, whose code name was Mina, nodded. It seemed all of the Team Four members had used their real names instead of code names.

"No one even knows if Ashton is a man or a woman," Mina said. She looked just as excited as Scott. "Oh my gosh! Can you believe we might actually be able to meet the author of Agent Ada? I'm so excited!"

"If you couldn't tell, we're the biggest Adamirers," Scott said. "But...I have to admit, we're not very good spies. I guess you could tell from our code names. We couldn't think of anything clever, so we just used our real names."

"I think your code names are great," Benny said. "At least you won't forget them."

Everyone laughed.

Everyone except Chameleon and the rest of Team Two, that is.

CONTINUE TO PAGE 41

RENDEZVOUS

Early the next morning, Henry and Violet showed Jessie and Benny the gadgets they'd been given for the competition: a drone with a camera, a tablet computer, two headsets, and a pair of mysterious glasses.

"We've also got these cool spy outfits to wear," Benny said, showing Henry and Violet the utility belts and black jackets that had been waiting in their rooms. "I can't wait to see what our challenge is. Do you think we'll sneak into a top secret meeting? Or maybe track down a villain?"

Henry chuckled. "Who knows, Benny? We'll have to wait and find out."

There was a knock on the door. A moment later, a white envelope was slipped under. Jessie picked it up and opened it.

"'Good morning, agents,'" she read. "'This morning you will have your first mission. It will take place in Chester Hills. Meet in the lobby at nine o'clock sharp. Bring only your tablet and the sunglasses, and dress in the most *normal* clothes you have.'"

"Normal clothes?" Benny asked. He wanted to wear his cool new spy jacket.

"That's all right, Agent Hot Dog," Henry said, using Benny's code name from the night before. "You can wear these. Dr. Sharpe, the technology lady, said someone from each team needed to have them on at all times. Think you can handle that?"

Benny nodded solemnly and then put the sunglasses on.

Jessie packed the tablet in her backpack. "Ready to go, Hot Dog, Amethyst, and Cluemaster?" she asked.

"Let's go, Professor J!" said Violet.

The members of Team Three were already waiting. Jessie waved hello to the two with the code names InfraRed and Gigabyte, who they had met at dinner the night before. InfraRed introduce the other two members of the team: Jumpdrive, a girl who looked to be about fifteen, and Wi-Fi, a boy about Violet's age with dark red hair and freckles.

"Jumpdrive, InfraRed, Wi-Fi, and Gigabyte," Violet whispered. "They all have technology names. I remember yesterday in the Gadgetry, Wi-Fi was great with the drone."

"We'll have to watch out for them when it comes to technology," Henry said.

A few minutes later, Team Two and Team Four entered the lobby. Scott, Mina, and the other two members of Team Four were still chattering about being in A.D. Ashton's house. It seemed not even a night's rest had dulled their excitement.

Chameleon, Leopard, and the other two members of Team Two kept to themselves on the other side of the lobby, away from everyone else. They seemed to be sizing up the competition.

"Do you think we're going to ride in a spy car like Agent Ada's?" Benny asked. "With the jet booster and the computer screen?"

Violet giggled. "I hope so. But probably not. I

think we're supposed to fit in to our surroundings on today's mission."

A honk sounded from outside, and all four teams stepped out into the cold. Parked on the driveway was a short school bus that reminded Violet of the kind she'd taken for field trips. She heard Benny give a little sigh and nudged him with her elbow.

"I know it's not a spy car," Violet said. "But think of it as a spy...bus!"

Benedict honked the horn again, and all sixteen children boarded the bus. Benedict closed the door, shutting out the chilly air. A moment later they were heading down the road.

Chester Hills was a short drive away. It was a small village with a main street filled with shops, many of which sold ski and sledding equipment for travelers who had come to visit the resorts. There were a few markets, a barbershop, and even a pet store with puppies and kittens playing in the window.

Benedict slowed the bus and opened the door. "Team One, this is your stop," he called.

Henry got up, and Jessie, Violet, and Benny followed him to the front of the bus. Just as they were about to step out, Benedict said, "Agents, remember to stick to the script."

Before they knew it, the Aldens were standing on the sidewalk as the bus drove away. They looked up and down Main Street. A gentle snow had begun to fall, lit by the bright morning sky.

"It's pretty bright out. I'm glad I'm wearing sunglasses," said Benny.

"Stick to the script, huh?" Henry repeated what Benedict had said. "Wonder what that means."

"And I wonder what we're supposed to do now," Violet said. "We weren't given any instructions at all, except that we'd need the tablet and the glasses."

Jessie wasn't worried. "Agent Ada doesn't always know what her secret missions are. I bet it's part of our job to figure it out."

"You're right," said Henry. He headed down the street at an easy walk. "Benedict dropped us off here for a reason. Let's see what's going on around us. Benny, are you coming?"

Henry, Jessie, and Violet turned back. Benny had fallen behind and was peering at the brick wall of one of the shops.

"I'm trying to read something," Benny said.

"But there's nothing there," Violet said. All she could see were the orange and red bricks.

"There is too," Benny said. "It says, 'The M-O-L-E...'"

"M-O-L-E?" Violet repeated. "Mole? Benny, where are you seeing those words?"

The Aldens gathered around where Benny was looking. Henry snapped his fingers.

"Aha! It's got to be those sunglasses," he said. "They were an important part of today's mission, remember? Benny's the only one who can see the letters because he's wearing the glasses— the message must be written in some kind of invisible ink!"

Jessie took the tablet out of her backpack and handed it to Violet, along with the writing stylus. "Here, Violet. Benny, spell out the letters you see, and Violet will write them down. Then we'll know what it says."

Benny did just that. Violet wrote down the letters Benny said, using the tablet the same way she might use a notebook and pencil. When they were done, they had a mysterious sentence written down: THE MOLE IS OUT OF THE BOX AND READY FOR THE RAIN.

"What does that mean?" Benny asked. "It's not raining; it's snowing. And what's a mole?"

"It's a little animal, kind of like a mouse or rat," Henry said.

"Do you think it might be a kind of pet animal?" Violet asked hopefully. "I saw a pet shop down the street when we first got into town. Do you think we should go there and see if there are any clues about what our secret mission is?"

"Good idea," Jessie said. "Let's walk that way."

The walk down Main Street was pleasant. The clouds and snow cleared, and the sun came out. It wasn't nearly as cold as the day before, so the Aldens were able to enjoy the walk, taking in the sights and the fresh mountain air. Benny looked around with his sunglasses but didn't see any more messages.

Violet tugged Jessie's sleeve. "Don't look now, but there's a man who looks a little suspicious across the street," she whispered.

The Great Spy Showdown

Jessie looked carefully. A man in a trench coat and a wide-brimmed hat sat on a bench in front of a theater. He had large sunglasses on, which covered almost all of his face. Jessie thought he looked just like an old-fashioned spy from some of the black-and-white movies Grandfather liked to watch. Jessie tapped Henry on the shoulder and whispered for him to look. Then he quietly told Benny what they'd seen.

"Over here," Henry said. He turned down an alley. From there, they were out of sight, but they could still see the man in the long coat.

"We're spying! We're spying!" Benny said.

"Do you think we're supposed to talk to him?" Jessie asked. "After all, he might not have anything to do with the competition. If that's the case, we shouldn't spy on him from an alley."

"Look—there's Scott and Team Four," Henry said. "Let's see what they do."

From the alley, the Aldens watched Scott, Mina, and the rest of Team Four walk up to the man in the trench coat. Scott held the tablet, but none of the four were wearing the sunglasses. Scott waved and said something, but the man did not respond. When Scott tried again, the man gave him a blank look and shook his head. It looked like the man didn't know what Scott wanted. And he didn't seem interested in having a conversation. After a few seconds, Scott and his teammates turned away, scratching their heads in confusion.

"It doesn't look like that went well," Henry said.

"Did you notice none of them were wearing the sunglasses?" Violet asked. "Maybe they forgot. Or misunderstood."

"Just like how they misunderstood making code names," Benny said. "If they didn't use the sunglasses, they probably didn't see any secret message about the hamster."

"*Mole*, Benny," said Violet with a grin.

"Well, team," Jessie began, "we've got a decision to make. We can try to talk to that man and see if we get different results than Team Four. Or, we can keep going to the pet shop to see if they know anything about the mole in the secret message. What do you think we should do?"

The Great Spy Showdown

IF THE ALDENS GO TO THE PET SHOP,
GO TO PAGE 52.

IF THE ALDENS SPEAK WITH THE MAN IN THE
TRENCH COAT, GO TO PAGE 59.

THE PET SHOP

"We already saw what happened when Team Four tried to talk to the man," Henry said. "And just because he's dressed like a spy doesn't mean that he is one. Let's go to the pet shop and see if they know anything about the mole."

The Aldens continued down the street toward the pet shop. On the way, they passed InfraRed and the rest of Team Three, who were headed in the opposite direction. Gigabyte was wearing the sunglasses. His goofy grin matched Benny's, and they high-fived as they passed.

"Good luck," Gigabyte said.

"You too!" said Benny.

After Team Three had passed, Violet sighed and wrung her hands nervously.

The Great Spy Showdown

"Do you think it's strange that they're going away from the pet shop?" she asked. "They'll pass the man in the trench coat soon if they keep going in that direction, and Gigabyte was wearing the glasses."

"Hmm, and from that smile on his face, I bet they found a secret message too," Jessie said. "Maybe they were already at the pet shop and found a clue. In that case, we should hurry up. I get the feeling all four teams are supposed to reach the same goal, and the last team to reach it will be eliminated."

"We're almost to the pet shop," Henry called from up ahead. "If we're wrong and need to talk to the man in the trench coat, we can go and talk to him after."

"I hope you're right," Violet said.

The pet shop door jangled as they entered, and inside was even louder. Parrots and parakeets chirped and sang and squawked. Hamsters and ferrets played in their pens, and near the window a half a dozen puppies yipped and yapped excitedly at the people walking by outside.

"Boy, it sure is loud," said Benny. He had to raise his voice just so the others could hear him.

"I'll go talk to the manager about the mole," Jessie shouted. She made her way through the parrot cages toward the counter, but there was a line. Jessie knew they were in a rush but did not want to draw attention to herself, so she waited.

Finally, she reached the front of the line. "Excuse me—" she began.

"What's that? I can't hear you!" said the woman, putting her hand around her ear.

Jessie hesitated. The shop was small. All the customers would hear her if she raised her voice. She did not want others to know about their mission. But if she didn't speak up, there was no way the manager would hear her over all the barking and yowling and squawking. She tried again, speaking a little louder.

"Excuse me, do you know anything about—" she began.

"Speak up, I still can't hear you!" the manager shouted.

Suddenly, Benny pulled off his glasses, stepped

up to the counter, and yelled, "Do you have any rats wearing raincoats!?"

The whole shop went quiet at his booming voice. The dogs stopped barking. The birds stopped squawking. Benny blushed and turned away from the counter when he realized everyone—even the animals—was staring at him. Embarrassed, he hurried out of the shop.

The manager looked confused. "I'm sorry, our rats don't wear raincoats," she said.

"What about...moles?" Jessie asked, but she had a feeling she already knew the answer.

"Moles? No one keeps moles as pets. That's just downright odd!" the manager said with a laugh. The cat sitting on her lap yowled, and a moment later, the birds started chirping and the dogs started barking.

"Oh dear," Jessie said. "Come on, Henry, Violet. Let's go after Benny."

Benny was outside. The grin was gone from his face, and he had taken off his sunglasses.

"I guess they don't have any moles," he said. "I didn't mean to yell like that. It was just so noisy."

The Great Spy Showdown

Benny handed Jessie the sunglasses, and Jessie put them on, hoping it might cheer him up. They looked sort of funny on her, and Benny cracked a little smile.

"It's all right, Benny," Henry said. "Either way, the pet shop was a dead end. Let's head back the other way. Maybe the man with the trench coat will still be there, and we can see if he knows anything about moles."

The four began the walk but halted when Jessie stopped in her tracks. She was looking down at the sidewalk with his sunglasses.

"Oh no," she said. There was a message written on the sidewalk. It looked like it was hastily written in chalk, but when Jessie peeked over the top of the sunglasses, she couldn't see anything. It was only visible through the glasses.

"What is it, Jessie? Another invisible message?" Violet asked.

"Yeah, but this one isn't good," Jessie said. "It says the other teams have completed their mission. Someone must have written it while we were in the pet shop..." She sighed, shaking her head.

"But who could have written it?" said Benny, looking around. "Do you think A.D. Ashton was here?"

"Either way, we're out of the competition," said Henry. "I guess it's time to call Grandfather and go home."

THE END

TO FOLLOW A DIFFERENT PATH, GO TO PAGE 51.

THE MAN IN THE TRENCH COAT

"The man in the trench coat is right across the street," Jessie said. "Let's try talking to him first, and if it seems like he isn't a part of the spy competition, we can go to the pet store."

"Make sure to mention the secret message you saw, Benny," Henry said.

"The mole is out of the box and..." Benny trailed off. "What was the other part?"

"Ready for the rain," Violet said. She showed him the tablet, where she'd written down the message.

"The mole is out of the box and ready for the rain," Benny said. "Okay, I got it... Hey, wait a minute. I see something."

Benny pointed across the alley. Some cardboard boxes were stacked there, folded up and ready for the recycling truck. Although the others couldn't see it, through the sunglasses, Benny could see words clear as day. Several sentences were written on the boxes, glowing white when he looked at them with the sunglasses.

"Some more messages?" Violet asked. She got the tablet and stylus ready. "Tell me what you see, Benny!"

Benny read the messages out loud, sounding out the words when he could and spelling the letters when he came to a word he didn't know. After a few minutes, Violet had written all of the sentences onto the tablet.

THE MOLE IS OUT OF THE BOX AND READY FOR THE RAIN.

THE EAGLE CAN SEE THE STORM FROM THE TOP OF A TREE.

FROM THE SPRUCE, WHAT DOES THE BIRD SEE?

"What does all this mean?" Violet asked. "It sounds like a riddle."

"It reminds me of a Shakespeare play," Jessie said.

That gave Henry an idea. "Remember what Benedict said when we got off the bus? He told us to stick to the *script*. Maybe that's what this is, a script."

"I think I get it," said Violet. "It's like in Agent Ada's adventure *The Turkey Has Landed*. When she tells another spy that 'the turkey has landed,' the other agent knows she is saying the bad guy had arrived."

"Oh, right!" Jessie said. "Spies use code words so their messages can't be understood by other people who might be listening."

"Come to think of it, I think I've heard the word *mole* used another way before," Henry said. "In some of Grandfather's old spy movies. I remember them calling an informant a *mole*. So this message probably isn't about an animal at all—it's about someone with information!"

"A mole who's ready for the rain because he's wearing a big coat!" said Benny.

"Team Four wasn't looking with their glasses on," Henry said as the Aldens crossed the street. "So they wouldn't know the script."

"But we do!" said Violet.

The Aldens approached the man sitting on the bench. Now that they were closer, they could see he had a bushy beard covering the part of his face that wasn't already hidden behind his big sunglasses. His trench coat collar was turned up, and his hands were in his pockets. He didn't look at the children as they approached.

"Remember, act normal," Jessie said. She put her hands in her pockets and whistled casually. They walked closer to the bench, and as they passed, Benny said to the man, "The mole is out of the box and ready for the rain."

The man did not turn his head. In fact, it almost looked like he had not heard Benny at all. But then, in a secretive voice, he said, "The eagle can see the storm from the top of a tree."

Benny opened his mouth to say the next line, but realized he had forgotten. Luckily, Violet had remembered.

"From the spruce, what does the bird see?" she asked.

"The mole's favorite flowers will grow beneath the spiral pole," the man said. Then he got up and walked away. When he was gone, Violet took out her tablet and made sure to write down what the man had said, so they wouldn't forget.

"Was that our clue?" Benny asked.

"Spiral pole," Jessie said. "Remember, when we first came to town? There was a barbershop at the other end of Main Street. I think it had a barber pole in front, by the window."

Henry grinned. "A spiral pole! Let's go!"

As the Aldens turned to go toward the barbershop, they caught sight of Chameleon, Leopard, and the rest of Team Two walking down the other side of the street. The youngest member of their group, Katydid, had the glasses on. The four spotted the man in the trench coat, who was still making his way down Main Street away from where he'd given the Aldens their clue.

The Aldens watched as Team Two crossed the street and approached the man. After a moment of conversation, the man in the trench coat walked away, and Team Two wrote something on their tablet.

"I think they just got the clue too," Henry said. "Come on. Let's get to the barbershop before they do. But let's not run, or it'll attract attention.

Remember, spies have to be secretive."

Henry led his siblings down Main Street. Benny tried not to look over his shoulder when Team Two started heading the same way.

"Either they figured out the clue, and they're headed to the barbershop too...or they're following us," Jessie said quietly.

"It's okay," Henry said. "We'll get there first. And anyway, only one team is eliminated in each round. As long as we don't get there last, we'll still make it to the next mission."

Even so, Benny yelped when Team Two broke into a run. All four of them passed on either side of the Aldens. Katydid even bumped into Violet.

"Sorry!" Katydid said, but she didn't sound sorry.

"Should we run?" Benny asked, grabbing Henry's hand. "They're going to win!"

"No, Benny," Henry said.

"Think about what Agent Ada would do," Jessie added. "There's no way Ada would go running down the street, bumping into people and making a scene like that."

Benny stood up straight. "You're right," he said.

The Great Spy Showdown

The Aldens reached the barbershop after a few minutes. It was an old-fashioned shop with a blue-and-red barber pole spinning in front of the main window. Team Two was nowhere to be seen.

"The mole's favorite flowers grow beneath the spiral pole," Violet said, remembering what the man in the trench coat had said. She checked the flower box in the windowsill below the barber pole. There were no flowers in it because it was wintertime. Instead, it was full of slushy, wet snow. Some of the snow was moved around.

"Looks like Team Two already got here," Henry said. "Find anything, Violet?"

"Yes!" Violet said. Hidden in the snow were two small plastic boxes.

"I bet there were three, and Team Two already got theirs," Jessie said. "Boy. They didn't have to run like that."

"What matters is we got here second," Henry said. "Violet, let's see what's inside. Be sure to leave the other box for the third team."

The Aldens took their box, carefully covering the last box with snow. They walked away from the barbershop, so they would not give away anything to the other teams. Then they opened the box.

Inside were four slides, like the ones Grandfather used in his slide reel to project photographs onto his projector screen. Even though they didn't have a screen, it was bright enough that they could see the pictures in the slides just by holding them up to the sky.

"Who are these people?" Benny asked.

"This looks like a photo of Benedict," Jessie said. "And this one is the painting of the woman hanging in the entryway of the manor."

"And this one is Dr. Sharpe," Henry said. "She explained how all the spy gadgets worked."

"And this...this is the man in the trench coat we just met," said Violet, looking at the fourth slide. "Why do you think these slides were in the little box?"

"Maybe they have something in common," said Henry. They packed the slides up, and Jessie put them in her backpack to keep them safe.

"I'm sure that's part of what we're supposed to figure out," Jessie said. "We can take a closer look when we get back to our home base."

"Look, here comes Team Three," Benny said.

The Aldens watched as Team 3, led by Jump-drive, approached the barbershop. Three of them stood back, keeping watch, while Wi-Fi checked the flower box under the barber pole. A moment later, all four of them walked away, as if nothing had happened.

"I guess that means Team Four is out," Henry said. "Too bad they didn't follow instructions and wear their glasses. They might have had a chance talking to that man in the trench coat."

"This is a competition after all," said a voice from behind them. They turned with a start and saw Benedict waving from the sidewalk. Over his shoulder was a bulky satchel. He was standing next to the parked bus.

"Hello, Benedict," Henry said. "We didn't hear you pull up."

"I must have picked up some of Agent Ada's spy techniques from working for so long with A.D. Ashton," said Benedict. "In any case, it looks as though this round has ended. Unfortunately, it seems Team Four will be eliminated. Come along, everyone. Back onto the bus and we'll return to the manor presently!"

He waved again and got onto the bus. As he did, something caught Violet's eye. It was the tail of a trench coat sticking out of Benedict's overstuffed satchel.

CONTINUE TO PAGE 69

RECOVERY

When they got back to the manor, the three remaining teams exited the bus.

"The next mission will begin this evening," Benedict said. "Until then, you're welcome to enjoy the manor property, so long as you remain in the areas discussed during the tour. Please report to the entryway at seven o'clock this evening, and prepare by bringing *all* of the gadgets you've been provided. You should also make use of the special gear provided in your rooms. Until then, *adieu*."

Violet and her siblings went up to their room. She was excited for a chance to try on the utility belt and jacket.

"There are so many pockets in this jacket," she said. "It would be neat if we win the competition and were able to keep all this spy gear. Just think about how we could use them on our other travels."

"I wonder what kind of challenge we'll have tonight," said Jessie. "By seven o'clock, it'll be pretty dark."

"Spies must be able to operate even in the darkest night," Henry said, using a voice like a secret agent. He chuckled afterward, which didn't sound very secret at all.

At seven o'clock, the Aldens arrived in the main entryway, dressed in their spy gear. Henry carried the case that contained the drone, the headsets, and the tablet. Benny still wore the sunglasses. He had not taken them off all day because he didn't want to miss any hidden messages.

Team Two and Team Three joined them. Violet tried not to worry too much about Team Two, even though Chameleon and Leopard looked intimidating dressed in their black spy gear with their serious faces.

"Chameleon, Leopard, Arctic Fox, and Katydid," said Wi-Fi, the member of Team Three who was just a little older than Violet. "I wonder how they chose their code names. My team chose code names that all had to do with technology... I guess because we're all a little geeky." He winked.

"Well, Team Two's code names are all animals," Violet said. She tilted her head. "You know, all four of those animals have really excellent camouflage. They're good at blending in to their surroundings. It's a skill that's very useful to a spy."

Wi-Fi raised both his eyebrows. "That's a great observation, Agent Amethyst," he said.

Violet smiled and tapped her temple with a finger. "Observation is another useful spy skill, after all!" she said.

The children fell quiet when Dr. Sharpe walked in. She was dressed in outdoor clothing: durable pants and a black coat similar to the ones the children were wearing. Her headset with the antenna was replaced by a tight black cap and a pair of goggles.

"Good evening, agents," she said. "Tonight your mission will be recovery. In real life, information can be stolen. If that happens, that data can fall into the wrong hands and put people in danger.

The Great Spy Showdown

Tonight's mission will test if your team has what it takes to recover stolen information. The first two teams to find and recover the information will advance to the next stage in the competition. The last team will be eliminated. Now, let us begin."

Dr. Sharpe spun on her heel and marched outside.

The sun had gone down, and the sky was dark blue. The wind was blustery, but Violet wasn't cold thanks to the cozy spy gear. Violet, her siblings, and the two other teams followed Dr. Sharpe around to the back of the manor, where dense trees grew from a hillside covered in snow. The snow itself was deep, almost up to Violet's knees. Walking through it wasn't easy.

"I will take each team to a separate starting point," Dr. Sharpe said. "When I blow my whistle, the mission begins. I offer you only one piece of advice: remember, a true spy can see equally well in the dark as in the day."

One at a time, Dr. Sharpe led the teams to spots along the edge of the woods. The Aldens' starting spot was near a big tree on the far side of the hill. From where the Aldens stood, Violet couldn't see the other teams, only the glittering snow shining in the moonlight. There they waited until they heard Dr. Sharpe's whistle. Once it blew, sharp and loud, they headed into the woods.

"Do we even know what we're looking for?" Henry asked. "I can hardly see anything in this dark... Benny, take those sunglasses off, they'll make it impossible for you to see where you're going."

But unlike Henry, Benny seemed to have no trouble walking in the dark. He easily found his way around the trees, stumps, and bushes at the forest's edge.

The other three Aldens looked at one another. Then Jessie gasped. "Benny, are those glasses helping you see in the dark?"

"I can see everything as clear as if it were daytime," Benny said, looking around. "Just like Dr. Sharpe said: 'A true spy can see well even in the dark!'"

"If they have the right glasses," said Henry, chuckling. "All right, Benny. Take a look around, and help us find whatever it is we're looking for."

Benny looked up and down, left and right.

The Great Spy Showdown

When he looked through the glasses, it was as if it wasn't nighttime at all. He could see the fluffy snow covering fallen logs and pine boughs. He could even see a strange-looking chest up ahead near a rock.

"There's something over there," he said, pointing.

The Aldens trudged through the snow to where Benny was pointing. The chest was almost as long as Benny was tall. Henry opened the lid, and inside they found eight objects made of wood and leather.

"What are those?" asked Benny. "They look like tennis rackets."

"Snowshoes!" Henry said. "These will make it easy for us to walk through the woods over the snow."

Henry showed Violet and Benny how to strap their boots into the snowshoes. Once the snowshoes were on, the children were able to walk on top of the snow, instead of through it.

"Paired with Benny's ability to see in the dark, suddenly this trek through the snowy woods is a lot easier," Jessie said.

"I see footprints leading that way," Benny said. "Should we follow them?"

The Great Spy Showdown

"I don't see why not," Henry said. "Lead the way."

Even with the snowshoes, it was slow going. And the Aldens had to stop more than once to take a break. Finally, Benny pointed through the darkness.

"I see something up ahead. It looks like a cabin or something," he said. "This way!"

Benny led them through the trees to a wooden shack that sat on top of a hill. Beyond the shack, the slope went from gentle to very steep. A pair of skis rested against the shack near the door, and there was a dim light on inside.

"The footprints turn into stripes here," Benny said. "I think they are skier tracks. Do you think we're supposed to start skiing?"

"Let's go inside first and see what's going on," Jessie suggested.

When the Aldens opened the door, they found Arctic Fox and Leopard from Team Two, as well as InfraRed, Jumpdrive, and Gigabyte from Team Three. Gigabyte and Arctic Fox both held the handsets for their drones. Violet remembered how good Gigabyte had been with the drone back in the Gadgetry. Was Arctic Fox good with it too?

"Where are Chameleon and Katydid?" Henry asked.

"And Wi-Fi," Violet added.

"Chameleon and Katydid are already on their way to winning this competition," Leopard said, tossing her ponytail. She had a headset on and was looking at her team's tablet.

"Wonder if it has to do with the skis," Jessie said. "If the others have already left, we've got to catch up. I'll take the last pair and head down the slope."

"Jessie, are you sure?" Henry asked.

"Yes. I'm a good skier. Benny, can I take the sunglasses so I can see where I'm going?" Jessie asked.

Benny nodded and handed the glasses to her. "But, Jessie, even with the glasses, how will you know where to go?" he asked.

"He's right. The hillside is covered in trees and rocks. Even if you can see in the dark, finding your way down at such a high speed is going to be dangerous," Henry said.

"Then you're going to guide me with the drone," Jessie said. She took one of the headsets out of their equipment case and handed the other to Violet. "Come on. We don't have time to lose!"

Violet nodded and took the tablet out. The other teams were already talking into their headsets, using the tablet and the drones to guide their team members. Henry warmed up the drone and walked outside with Jessie.

"Good luck!" he said. "And be careful."

"Thanks," Jessie said. She put on ski boots, skis, and the glasses. "And I will!"

Violet sat with the tablet inside the cabin. A moment later, the camera feed from the drone showed up on the screen. The video feed was bright and easy to see.

"Looks like the drone has night vision too," Henry said. "All right. Let's see what I can do."

Henry used the handset to control the drone, sending it up into the air. From the drone's camera feed, Violet could see Jessie taking off down the slope on her skis.

"Good thing Jessie's such a good skier," Benny said.

"Especially since she has to catch up with the

other teams," said Henry.

"Jessie, are you there?" Violet asked into the headset.

Violet could hear Jessie's voice clearly when she replied, "I hear you, Violet! Tell me where to go."

Violet watched the screen while Henry flew the drone. She could see Jessie whizzing down the slope, expertly swooping left and right. When Violet saw trees or rocks from the drone's camera feed, she told Jessie right away.

"Rock coming up on your left, Jessie—look out!"

Jessie easily turned to the right. Then to the left and to the right again, avoiding the obstacles as Violet guided her. Snow flew up from Jessie's skis as she blew down the slope.

"What's that?" Violet gasped.

Figures became visible up ahead. From the drone's camera, Violet could make out three figures on skis, all dressed in black spy gear. Two of the skiers—Chameleon and Katydid—were ganging up on Wi-Fi. Both of the Team Two members were much bigger than Wi-Fi, who wasn't much bigger than Violet. They used their weight to push him back and forth, trying to knock him down even as they raced down the steep, slippery slope.

Chameleon elbowed Wi-Fi hard, finally sending him tumbling into a snowbank. The two members of Team Two sped past, ignoring the trouble they'd caused.

Jessie was close enough that she had seen the whole thing. She was coming up to the place where Wi-Fi had landed after being knocked over. It had been a big crash.

"Wi-Fi might be hurt," Jessie said into the headset. "But if I stop to check on him, we could lose the competition. What should I do?"

IF JESSIE CHASES AFTER CHAMELEON AND KATYDID,
GO TO PAGE 81.

IF JESSIE STOPS TO HELP WI-FI,
GO TO PAGE 85.

GIVING CHASE

"I think I can beat Chameleon and Katydid to the bottom if I keep going," Jessie said. She didn't try to slow down, passing by the place where Wi-Fi had fallen in the snow.

"Jessie, if you go too fast, the drone won't be able to keep up," Violet said. "Henry's already having trouble with the propellers because of the cold air!"

"Then I'll have to do it without the drone's help," Jessie said. "I just hope Wi-Fi is okay."

Jessie bent her knees and braced herself, trying to see ahead. Even though the glasses helped her see in the dark, the snow flurries were getting stuck to the lenses, and everything was going by so quickly. She could almost see the two members of Team Two up ahead.

"Jessie, slow down—we lost you with the drone," Violet said.

Jessie looked up. The drone was no longer above her.

"Oh no…"

Jessie looked down and gasped. A big mound of snow raced up on her. Before she could swerve around it, she went up and over it, losing her balance and flying into the air. One of her skis came off and spun away, just before she landed in a big pillow of fresh powder.

"Jessie, are you okay?" Violet asked over the headset.

"Yes, I'm fine," Jessie said, standing up. She groaned with disappointment when she realized what had happened. "But I'm afraid I lost one of my skis."

Jessie turned at a sound coming from behind her. A moment later, Wi-Fi skied by, carefully moving down the slope after Chameleon and Katydid. It seemed he was okay after his tumble, and now he was on his way to the bottom. Unlike Jessie. Even with the night vision glasses and the drone's camera, there was no way she was going to find her missing ski in time.

"Sorry," she said. "Looks like we're going home this round."

THE END

TO FOLLOW A DIFFERENT PATH, GO TO PAGE 80.

JESSIE STOPS TO HELP

"I'm going to stop and make sure Wi-Fi's okay!" Jessie said.

She turned, and a fan of snow sprayed up as she slid to a halt near the mound of snow where Wi-Fi had landed. He was sitting up, holding his ankle with a grimace on his face.

"Are you all right?" Jessie asked, getting closer. It wasn't easy to move around on the skis, but she had to make sure he wasn't hurt.

"I think I sprained my ankle," said Wi-Fi. "Those two bullies really pulled a number on me. I dropped one of my ski poles, and my glasses fell off...I bet Team Two is all the way to the bottom of the hill by now."

"This isn't a time to worry about the competition," Jessie said. "I'll try and find your things. Wait here."

It wasn't easy searching in the dark, but Jessie managed to find the ski pole sticking out of a snowbank, and Henry used the drone to spot the glasses dangling from a tree branch. Jessie brought the items back to Wi-Fi.

"Thanks, Professor J," Wi-Fi said.

"No problem. Now let's see if you can stand," said Jessie.

She helped Wi-Fi up, but he winced and groaned when he tried to put weight on his hurt ankle.

"I don't think it's broken, but I don't think I should ski the rest of the way down either," Wi-Fi said. "I'm going to have to have my team call for help to get back to the manor."

"I'll wait with you," Jessie said.

"No," said Wi-Fi. "You should keep going. If you don't, Team Two will win automatically. That wouldn't be right, not after what bullies they've been. I'll be fine waiting here. I want you to go and advance in the competition."

"Are you sure?" Jessie asked.

The Great Spy Showdown

Wi-Fi gave her an encouraging smile. "I'm sure," he said. "Thanks again for helping me. Now, go!"

Jessie nodded and gave him a salute. Then she tightened her grip on her poles and continued on down the slope.

"Jessie, can you hear me?" Violet asked over the headset. "InfraRed and Team Three are going to help us with their drone! Listen carefully. I think we've found the best way down."

Jessie listened to Violet's instructions. She cut sharply to the left, where the trees suddenly opened up into a smooth hill. Jessie could see the lights of another cabin at the bottom. Thanks to Violet's instructions and the two drones, she made it to the foot of the slope within minutes. As soon as she arrived, she took off her skis and went inside.

Chameleon and Katydid were already there, standing at the wood table in the center of the room.

"So you made it after all," Chameleon said. "I guess it'll be your team we'll beat in the final mission."

He took an envelope that was on the table and

tossed it to Jessie, who picked it up and opened it. Inside was a simple note card that read *Mission Accomplished*. Accompanying the card was a single photograph, which showed a person standing in front of the Ashton Manor, but the person's face had been cut out of the picture. Jessie put the photo in the front pocket of her jacket to keep it safe until she could share it with Henry, Violet, and Benny.

The sound of an engine came from outside. Jessie followed Chameleon and Katydid outside to find Dr. Sharpe on a big four-wheeler.

"Teams One and Two, eh?" Dr. Sharpe called as they took their seats on the four-wheeler's trailer. "Hmm...interesting. Well, I suppose we will see where this leads tomorrow in the final mission. In the meantime, let's go pick up Agent Wi-Fi and get back to the manor."

CONTINUE TO PAGE 89

MIDNIGHT SNACK

Dr. Sharpe brought the three teams back to the manor, and the Aldens said good-bye to Team Three. Afterward, Dr. Sharpe met with the Aldens and Team Two in the entryway.

"You've had a long day, so dinner will be served in your rooms this evening. Rest up. Tomorrow is the final mission," Dr. Sharpe said.

When the Aldens returned to their room, they closed the door and changed into their comfy pajamas. The black spy outfits were cool, but they were wet with snow from being outside. It was nice to be indoors in the warmth. A tray with warm sandwiches was waiting for them.

"Oof, I'm sore," Jessie said after they ate, stretching out her arms and legs. "I'm going to soak in the bath for a bit. While I do, you three might want to take a look at the photo in the envelope I found at the bottom of the hill. See if you can make heads or tails of it."

Henry, Violet, and Benny sat on one of the beds and looked at the photograph. Benny still wore his glasses, but even he couldn't make any sense of the clue. The only thing the three of them noticed that Jessie hadn't was that the person in the photograph was holding a ring of keys.

"I've seen photos like this before," Henry said. "When people buy houses, they sometimes celebrate by taking a photo of themselves in front of their new house, holding their keys."

"Do you think this person was the owner of the Ashton Manor at some point?" Jessie asked.

"I'm not sure. But I'm sure we'll figure it out soon enough," said Henry. "Let's leave it alone for now and try to get some rest. We have an important challenge tomorrow."

"We're going head-to-head with Team Two," Violet reminded them. "I really don't like how they cheated when they bullied Wi-Fi on the slope tonight."

"Agent Ada would not have done that," Benny said. "They're mean."

"Violet, do you remember what you overheard them talking about in the Gadgetry, when they were accidentally broadcasting on the open channel?" Henry asked.

"Yes. They said something about how they needed to take a photograph with A.D. Ashton when they win. It was part of some kind of plan," Violet said.

Henry frowned, tapping his chin. "I wonder what they're up to. Let's just hope it doesn't end with someone getting hurt again."

***

Later that night, Benny woke up to a sound. It sounded like floorboards squeaking. When he heard it a second time, he put on his spy glasses so he could see in the dark and tapped Violet, who was sleeping in the bed next to his.

"Shh," he said. "Do you hear that?"

Violet nodded. "Sounds like someone walking around...but it's so late. Where could they be going?"

The Great Spy Showdown

Benny and Violet opened the door into the common area. The lights were on, but no one was in the room. Violet tiptoed across the room in her stocking feet. When she stepped on one part of the floor, it squeaked. The board was right in front of the room that was Team Two's.

"There was definitely someone walking around out here," she said. "And it looks like it was someone from Team Two."

"Maybe they're going to the kitchen for a midnight snack," said Benny. His stomach rumbled. "I think we should too. We don't want them to have more energy than us tomorrow."

"I don't think that's where they went," Violet said with a little smile. "Okay, Benny. We can either go to the kitchen to see if we can find a snack, or we can try to find Team Two and figure out why they're sneaking around in the middle of the night. But we can't do both."

Benny looked down the hall. His tummy grumbled...

The Great Spy Showdown

IF VIOLET AND BENNY TRY TO FIND THE MEMBERS OF TEAM TWO, GO TO PAGE 94.

IF VIOLET AND BENNY HEAD TO THE KITCHEN FOR A SNACK, GO TO PAGE 97.

FOLLOWING THE NOISE

"I think we should try to follow Team Two," Benny said. "They could be cheating again."

Violet nodded. "Good idea. Let's see if we can find out what they're up to. But we'll have to be quiet. Have your spy glasses ready."

Violet and Benny tiptoed downstairs. They didn't see anything, but Violet heard whispering. It was coming from the dark hallway that led to the east wing. She exchanged a glance with Benny in the dark. Then she crossed her hands at the wrists, making an X with her arms and shaking her head firmly. Agent Ada had done that once on an adventure where she and a partner had to sneak through a building without being heard. The X meant *no*.

Benny understood. Violet was reminding him that they were not supposed to be in the east wing. It was A.D. Ashton's living area.

They heard more whispering, then a metallic clinking sound. Violet pointed to Benny's glasses, and he put them on. When he did, he covered his mouth to keep from gasping. With the glasses, he could see right down the dark hallway. As clear as day, he saw Chameleon and Leopard trying to pick the lock of a closed door!

"I'm sure there will be evidence of A.D. Ashton's real identity in here," Chameleon whispered. "Can you imagine what kind of attention we'll get when we reveal his true identity?"

"It might go viral," said Leopard with a big smile. "We'll be famous!"

Another noise, this one like pots and pans in the kitchen, echoed down the quiet manor halls. Chameleon stopped picking the lock, and Violet and Benny ducked around a corner.

"We won't be famous if we get caught," Chameleon whispered. "Come on. We'll have to try again later."

The Great Spy Showdown

The two of them snuck away, heading back upstairs to their home base. In their hurry, they didn't see Benny and Violet hiding in the dark.

Violet frowned. She signaled to Benny, pointing back to the stairs, and the two slipped away from the dark hallway and hurried back to their room.

"We have to tell Jessie and Henry about this first thing in the morning," Violet said. "But for now, let's get some rest. Tomorrow is going to be a big day."

CONTINUE TO PAGE 102

THE KITCHEN

"If Team Two is up to no good, I don't want to be any part of it," Benny said. "Let's go find a snack and go back to bed."

Violet nodded. The two of them went downstairs toward the kitchen. The lamps on the main floor were turned on, so Benny didn't need to use his spy glasses. When Benny and Violet entered the dining hall, they heard the sound of pots and pans clinking in the kitchen.

"Oh good, someone's awake," Violet said. "Maybe they can help us get a snack."

Benny and Violet pushed open the swinging door that led from the dining hall into the kitchen. Dr. Sharpe was inside with her back turned to them. She was looking in the refrigerator and humming gently to herself.

"Hello, Dr. Sharpe!" Benny said cheerfully.

At the sound of Benny's voice, Dr. Sharpe jumped a foot off the ground and shouted, "*Sacrebleu!*" in a deep voice. She turned and sighed with relief when she saw Benny and Violet. "Forgive me, *monsieur, madame*," she said, still in a deep voice. "You surprised me."

Violet tilted her head. "Dr. Sharpe, you sound like Benedict. Why are you talking like that?" she asked.

Dr. Sharpe looked down at herself, and her eyes got wide, almost as though she was surprised to see what she was wearing. "Oh, excuse me," she said in her normal voice. "Benedict has been teaching me French. I was practicing. What brings you two to the kitchen?"

Benny was about to tell Dr. Sharpe about wanting a snack, but then they heard a distant crash from somewhere in the manor.

"What was that?" Violet asked.

Dr. Sharpe frowned. "I don't know. But it was coming from the east wing, which is off-limits."

The Great Spy Showdown

Dr. Sharpe marched out of the kitchen. Benny and Violet forgot about their snacks and followed her.

They went down the hall into the east wing of the manor, which Benedict had warned them against exploring. Halfway down the hall, they found a heavy door hanging open. The doorframe was in splinters. Someone had kicked it open and broken the lock.

"What's going on in here?" Dr. Sharpe said, storming into the room and turning on the lights. As soon as the lights came on, Benny and Violet could see inside. It was an office with bookcases and a writing desk, and in the middle of it were Chameleon and Leopard. They froze where they were, hoping they could disappear. They had been rummaging through the desk when Dr. Sharpe came in.

"Benedict strictly forbade everyone from exploring this part of the manor," Dr. Sharpe said. "And not only did you ignore his wishes, but you broke into A.D. Ashton's writing room. This is beyond unacceptable. I'm sorry, but for this, the competition must be canceled. Everyone return to your rooms. You will go home tomorrow. There will not be a winner."

THE END

TO FOLLOW A DIFFERENT PATH, GO TO PAGE 93.

ESCAPE

The next morning the Aldens woke to an envelope slipped under the door. It contained the instructions for the last mission.

"We'll be up against Team Two today," Henry said.

Benny gasped. "That reminds me," he said. "Last night, we saw Chameleon and Leopard trying to pick the lock to one of the off-limits rooms in the east wing. We were too sneaky though, and they didn't see us."

"But they were saying some really suspicious things," Violet said. "I think they came here in order to meet A.D. Ashton and reveal his true identity to the public."

"What? That's horrible," said Jessie.

The Great Spy Showdown

"Then they're not really fans of Agent Ada or A.D. Ashton at all," Henry said. "If they were, they'd know how important it is not to reveal secret identities. We'll just have to make sure to win the competition then. It's the only way to make sure they're not able to meet the author and reveal his true identity. Let's see what our instructions are for today."

Henry opened the envelope and read the note out loud: "'Agents: Today's final mission will be an indoor operation. Please meet Benedict by the east wing at nine o'clock, and bring only one gadget of your choosing.'"

"Only one gadget," Violet repeated. "Which one should we bring?"

Jessie looked across their gadgets—the two headsets, the sunglasses, the tablet, and the drone. "We have no idea what kind of mission this will be," she said. "Which of these gadgets has been the most useful?"

"The glasses!" Benny said. "They show hidden messages, and I can see in the dark."

"I think Benny's right. Plus, the instructions say

the mission is indoors. We probably won't need the drone," Violet said.

"And instead of the tablet, we can always use pen and paper," Jessie added.

"All right, it's settled then," Henry said. "Let's go meet Benedict."

The Aldens went downstairs to the east wing. Benedict was waiting there when they arrived. A few moments later, Team Two joined them. Chameleon and Leopard had dark circles under their eyes, as if they had been up late. Arctic Fox was holding the drone, the gadget his team had decided to take.

"Good morning, agents," Benedict said. "This way, please."

Benedict led them down the east wing hall for the first time. It looked similar to the west wing, where the Aldens had been staying. Benedict stopped in front of a pair of doors on the same side of the hall.

"Spies must be skilled in entering locked rooms unnoticed, but they must be equally skilled in getting out," Benedict said. "Team One, you will be in this room. Team Two, you will be in the room next door. I will lock the doors once you are inside. You will have half an hour to find the *key*. The team that succeeds first will be the winner of the Great Spy Showdown. If neither team finds the key before time runs out, then there will be no winner. Are you ready?"

All eight children nodded. Chameleon gave Henry a challenging look.

"Hope you're ready to lose," he said with a smile. Then he led his team into their room.

"One last bit of advice," Benedict said, raising an eyebrow at Chameleon. "If you find yourself at a crossroads, ask yourselves what Agent Ada would do. Good luck."

The Aldens went into their room. A moment the lock click.

"They hear just like the escape room game we played with Grandfather and Mrs. McGregor," Benny said once they were inside.

The room was not very big. It looked like an office or a study, with bookshelves along the walls and heavy red curtains on both sides of the tall windows. On the wall was a clock counting down from thirty minutes.

"All right, Team Boxcar," Henry said. "We don't have much time, so let's start looking for clues."

The four of them split up in the small room. Benny pulled his glasses down over his eyes. Violet investigated the bookshelf while Jessie took a look through the writing desk in the corner. On the desk were some pens and paper.

"Where does that door go?" Violet asked. There was a second door in the room, just visible between two bookcases.

"Probably into the room where Team Two is," Henry said. He tried the knob, but it was locked. "A lot of old manors have doors that go between rooms like this."

"Check this thing out," Benny said. was looking at a mechanical contraption sitting on a small table. Jessie brightened with excitement when she saw it.

"Benny! Do you know what that is?" Jessie asked. She took out the slides they had gotten at the end of their first challenge. "It's an old slide projector!

Henry, pull the curtains shut, would you? I'll bet this is a clue!"

The slides sitting next to the projector appeared to be blank, so Jessie instead put in the slides they had found during their mission. With the heavy curtains covering the windows, the room was quite dark. Light streamed out of one end of the projector, showing the first slide on the wall. It was a photograph of Benedict, as they had thought.

"He looks so serious," Violet said.

Jessie flipped to the next slide. It was a photograph of Dr. Sharpe. The next was a photo of the man in the trench coat from the first mission. "We've already looked at these, but it sure is easier to see them when they're blown up big like this," Jessie said.

"Hey, do you see that?" Benny asked. He pointed at the wall. The other Aldens did not see anything special.

"It must be more marks only you can see with the glasses," said Henry. "What is it?"

"It's a glowing circle on the wall. Right there, under the trench coat man's pocket," Benny said.

He took off his glasses and pointed again.

Now that the image was so much bigger, Violet could see details she hadn't been able to see before.

"There's a key hanging out of his pocket," Violet said.

"Benedict said we were looking for a *key* in these rooms," Henry said. "I thought he meant to unlock the door, but maybe it's more than that. Maybe the key is the answer to what ties all of these people in the photographs together."

"Change to the other slides," Violet said. "Let's see if we can find more keys."

The Aldens slowly flipped through the slides. Sure enough, Benedict the butler was holding a ring of keys in his hand, and Dr. Sharpe had an earring shaped like a key. Even the woman in the peach dress had a key dangling like a charm from her opera glasses. When they compared the keys in all four photographs, the children saw that the keys were all the same.

"What does it mean?" Benny asked.

Jessie took out the photograph she'd retrieved from the ski cabin the night before. "The face of

the owner of the manor is cut out," she said. "But the person is holding the same key as all of these other people."

"Do you think that means that all of these people own the mansion?" asked Benny.

"That's a good idea, Benny," said Jessie. "I think it does mean that. And I think it means something more too: I think they are all the same person! Think about it. We have only met three adults this whole time: Benedict, Dr. Sharpe, and the man in the trench coat."

"And when Benedict picked us up after our first mission, he had a bag that looked like it had a trench coat inside," said Violet. "I bet he was the man dressed as the mole too!"

"But if there is only one person at Ashton Manor," said Henry, "that means Benedict, Dr. Sharpe, and the mole are really..."

"A.D. Ashton!" Benny and Violet said together.

The children looked once more at all four of the slides. The person in each of the images had the same slight smile on their lips, as if they were keeping a very important secret. Now that the children were looking, the similarities were impossible to ignore.

"Wow," Violet gasped. "Ashton really *is* a master of disguise. Just like Agent Ada."

"You know what this means?" Henry said. "We've already met the author of Agent Ada—four different times!"

The Aldens jumped at a knocking sound. It was coming from the door that connected their room to Team Two's.

"Hey. Team One. You in there?" It was Leopard's voice.

The Aldens moved closer to the door.

"Yes?" Henry asked. "What is it?"

"We've got a clue. But we think it's only half of a clue. We thought maybe you had the other half."

Jessie looked at the projection on the wall, the photographs, and the slides. She glanced at Henry with uncertainty, then said through the door, "What kind of clue?"

"It's a message, but it's in some kind of code," Leopard said. "I think the clue to decoding it must be on your side. I'll make a copy and pass it over if you tell us what you've found."

They heard Chameleon's gruff voice next. "And if we win, we'll give you credit when we reveal A.D. Ashton's identity to the world," he said.

"Hey! Don't tell them about that!" Katydid called from the background.

"Just a minute," Henry said. He signaled to Jessie, Violet, and Benny to move away from the door, where they could talk without Chameleon and Leopard hearing them. "What do you think? We're almost out of time. We might know that Benedict, Dr. Sharpe, and A.D. Ashton are the same person, but we don't know how to unlock the door to escape the room. Team Two might be able to help us."

"But if we trade our information for theirs, they could win," Violet said. "And if they do, they're going to reveal A.D. Ashton's true identity to the world."

"But if we don't work with them, we might lose the competition," Benny said, frowning.

"We might lose the competition," Jessie said. "But remember, Benny: We know now that we've already met the author plenty of times, as Benedict and as

Dr. Sharpe. Isn't that what we wanted to do?"

"Well," Henry said, "we have to make a big decision. What should we do?"

IF THE ALDENS KEEP THEIR CLUE TO THEMSELVES,
GO TO PAGE 114.

IF THE ALDENS WORK WITH TEAM TWO,
GO TO PAGE 116.

KEEPING THE SECRET

"Benedict said we should ask ourselves what Agent Ada would do," Violet said. "Remember? And I know what Agent Ada would say about this: 'A spy should never reveal another spy's secret identity.' And that's just what Team Two is going to do. I don't think we should work with them."

"I agree," said Jessie. "I'd rather lose the competition than help them reveal A.D. Ashton's true identity."

Henry nodded. He went back to the door. "Sorry," he said to Team Two. "But if you're going to go through with your plan, you'll have to do it without our help."

The Aldens waited for the clock to count down. If they didn't work together with Team Two, there wasn't any way for them to get out of the room before time was up. Jessie rubbed Benny's back.

"It's all right," she told him. "We had a great time in the competition, didn't we? And we were finalists too."

"And we did the right thing," Henry added. "Just wait until Grandfather hears about all we did this weekend—invisible messages and seeing in the dark and Jessie's cool ski chase down the slope."

Benny nodded. "We *did* get to eat avocado toast and tomato soup right in A.D. Ashton's fancy manor."

The clock on the wall rang.

The competition was over.

CONTINUE TO PAGE 118

WORKING WITH THE ENEMY

"Even if we share our information, I think we can still beat Team Two," Henry said. "We have the sunglasses, but they brought the drone. We'll just have to be faster at decoding the message than they are."

The Aldens went back to the door. Henry knocked again.

"All right, we're going to tell you what we found out," he said. "But you should share your information first."

"Not going to happen," Chameleon said. "How about we both write our information down on paper, and slide the paper under the door at the same time?"

That sounded fair. Jessie found a pencil and

a piece of paper on the writing desk and wrote down what they had learned from the slides and the photographs: That A.D. Ashton, Benedict the Butler, and Dr. Sharpe were all the same person. She folded the paper and handed it to Henry.

"On the count of three," Henry said. He counted and slipped the paper under the door. At the same time, Leopard slipped their clue to the Aldens. Henry frowned.

"What does it say?" Benny asked.

"Nothing," Henry said. "It's blank. They fooled us."

The clock on the wall chimed. Time was up, and the Aldens had lost the competition.

THE END

TO FOLLOW A DIFFERENT PATH, GO TO PAGE 113.

A NEW CHAPTER

CLICK.

The door unlocked, and Benedict opened it. The Aldens followed him into the hallway, where Team Two was waiting. From the frustrated expressions on Chameleon's and Leopard's faces, Jessie guessed they hadn't been able to solve the escape room mystery either.

"Looks like no one's the winner," Violet said.

"If you had just shared your clue with us, we could have all been winners," Arctic Fox said. "Now we're all losers. Come on, guys, let's go home."

The two teams went to their rooms to get ready to go home. The Aldens arranged for Grandfather to come and pick them up.

By the time they had packed and brought their

suitcases to the entryway, the members of Team Two had already left. The manor was quiet, as if there was no one there but the Aldens.

"I wonder where Benedict went," said Henry. "I would have liked to thank him for everything. Especially now that we know who he *really* is."

"Grandfather says he'll be here soon," Jessie said, looking at the text message on her phone. "Maybe we can find Benedict or Dr. Sharpe to say good-bye before then."

"No need. I'm here," said a voice.

The Aldens turned to see a middle-aged woman enter from the east wing hallway. She was tall, like Benedict and Dr. Sharpe, and she wore a peach-colored sweater like the woman in the painting above the stairs. And like the woman in the painting, she had a secret little smile on her lips. Dangling around her neck was a necklace with a pendant in the shape of a key.

"A.D. Ashton!" said Benny. "Is it really you?"

The woman smiled. "It is really me, Hot Dog," she said. "Did you think I would let you leave without saying hello? It's why you entered the competition, isn't it?"

"But we didn't win," Violet said.

"Oh, but you did!" said the woman. "Come to my study. I want to show you something."

The Aldens followed the author down the hallway. She used the key on her necklace to unlock a door to a beautiful study full of books. Manuscripts were stacked in orderly piles on the desk. While the Aldens looked around, the author explained.

"My real name is Ashley Birmingham," she said. "When I was young, I worked as a spy for the government. That's why I use a pen name when I write books now."

Benny and Violet gazed at a wall full of photos. They were like the ones in the slides, but there were many more. When Violet looked closer, she saw the person in each photograph looked a little bit like Ms. Birmingham.

"These are all you, aren't they?" said Violet.

"Yes. Those are some of my favorite disguises," Ms. Birmingham said. "Listen, Henry, Jessie. Violet, Benny. Now that you know Benedict and Dr. Sharpe, as well as the mole in the trench coat, were all me, you have probably also guessed the truth. Which is that I have been keeping a very close eye on the entire competition. I knew that Chameleon, Leopard, and the rest of Team Two were planning to reveal my identity. That's why I arranged the final mission the way I did."

"You mean with the two clues?" Henry said. "I was really curious what information Team Two had in their room that they needed help with."

Ms. Birmingham chuckled. "Oh, they just had a letter with a bunch of gibberish writing on it and instructions to ask you for help decoding it," she said. "I had already decided I would disqualify them because of their plan to expose my identity. But I still wanted them to ask you for help, because I wanted to see what you would do. You see, I needed to know if I could trust the four of you."

"Of course you can trust us," Jessie said. "When we found out what they were planning, we knew we couldn't help them."

"Why did you need to know if you could trust the winners?" Benny asked. "Because you need to keep your identity a secret?"

The Great Spy Showdown

"Indeed," Ms. Birmingham said with a nod. "But for another reason too. You see, I decided to put on the Great Spy Showdown because it was fun, but I also was hoping to find young people who were trustworthy enough to do something very important for me."

"And what's that?" Henry asked.

Ms. Birmingham walked over to her desk and picked up one of the stacks of paper. She faced the Aldens and held it out to them.

"I was hoping to ask you the favor of reading the newest Agent Ada book," she said. "I can tell that problem solving and doing the right thing is important to all of you and that you truly understand the Agent Ada books. I can't think of anyone better to read my new manuscript first."

All four Aldens lit up. Violet took the manuscript carefully.

"We'd be honored!" she said.

A horn beeped outside. It sounded like the horn on Grandfather's car. Violet put the manuscript in her backpack, where it would be safe, and the Aldens went out to the front driveway. Ms.

Birmingham brought out the spy gear, which the children had won. Grandfather was waiting, cheeks rosy.

"Good morning, children!" he called with a wave.

Grandfather and Henry packed the car. When they were ready to go, they all said good-bye to Ms. Birmingham.

"We can't wait to read the manuscript," Jessie said. "Thank you so much."

"Thank *you* for taking the time to read it," said Ms. Birmingham. "I can't wait to hear what you think of it. Have a safe drive back home, and I'll look forward to hearing from you soon!"

Just as they were getting into the car, Benny paused.

"Wait a minute," he said. He thought of all the photographs in the study, and of Ms. Birmingham's many disguises. "How do we know Ashley Birmingham is your real name? Maybe you're in a disguise right now!"

Ms. Birmingham raised a finger to her lips and gave one of her secretive, little smiles.

"Maybe I am," she said with a wink. "One of

these days, I might slip up. My fingers aren't as nimble as they used to be, after all!"

Benny tilted his head. "I think I've heard that before," he said. For some reason, it made him think of the bookshop where they'd first gotten their invitation to the Great Spy Showdown.

Then Grandfather beeped the horn on the car, and they were off, driving down the sunny road where not a cloud was in sight.

THE END

TO FOLLOW A DIFFERENT PATH, GO TO PAGE 113.

Add to Your
Boxcar Children Collection!

The first twelve books are now available in
three individual boxed sets!

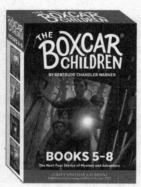

978-0-8075-0854-1 · US $24.99   978-0-8075-0857-2 · US $24.99   978-0-8075-0840-4 · US $24.99

The Boxcar Children Bookshelf includes the first twelve
books, a bookmark with complete title checklist,
and a poster with activities.

978-0-8075-0855-8 · US $69.99

THE BOXCAR CHILDREN MYSTERIES

THE BOXCAR CHILDREN
SURPRISE ISLAND
THE YELLOW HOUSE MYSTERY
MYSTERY RANCH
MIKE'S MYSTERY
BLUE BAY MYSTERY
THE WOODSHED MYSTERY
THE LIGHTHOUSE MYSTERY
MOUNTAIN TOP MYSTERY
SCHOOLHOUSE MYSTERY
CABOOSE MYSTERY
HOUSEBOAT MYSTERY
SNOWBOUND MYSTERY
TREE HOUSE MYSTERY
BICYCLE MYSTERY
MYSTERY IN THE SAND
MYSTERY BEHIND THE WALL
BUS STATION MYSTERY
BENNY UNCOVERS A MYSTERY
THE HAUNTED CABIN MYSTERY
THE DESERTED LIBRARY MYSTERY
THE ANIMAL SHELTER MYSTERY
THE OLD MOTEL MYSTERY
THE MYSTERY OF THE HIDDEN PAINTING
THE AMUSEMENT PARK MYSTERY
THE MYSTERY OF THE MIXED-UP ZOO
THE CAMP-OUT MYSTERY
THE MYSTERY GIRL
THE MYSTERY CRUISE
THE DISAPPEARING FRIEND MYSTERY
THE MYSTERY OF THE SINGING GHOST
THE MYSTERY IN THE SNOW
THE PIZZA MYSTERY
THE MYSTERY HORSE
THE MYSTERY AT THE DOG SHOW
THE CASTLE MYSTERY
THE MYSTERY OF THE LOST VILLAGE
THE MYSTERY ON THE ICE
THE MYSTERY OF THE PURPLE POOL
THE GHOST SHIP MYSTERY
THE MYSTERY IN WASHINGTON, DC
THE CANOE TRIP MYSTERY
THE MYSTERY OF THE HIDDEN BEACH
THE MYSTERY OF THE MISSING CAT
THE MYSTERY AT SNOWFLAKE INN

THE MYSTERY ON STAGE
THE DINOSAUR MYSTERY
THE MYSTERY OF THE STOLEN MUSIC
THE MYSTERY AT THE BALL PARK
THE CHOCOLATE SUNDAE MYSTERY
THE MYSTERY OF THE HOT AIR BALLOON
THE MYSTERY BOOKSTORE
THE PILGRIM VILLAGE MYSTERY
THE MYSTERY OF THE STOLEN BOXCAR
THE MYSTERY IN THE CAVE
THE MYSTERY ON THE TRAIN
THE MYSTERY AT THE FAIR
THE MYSTERY OF THE LOST MINE
THE GUIDE DOG MYSTERY
THE HURRICANE MYSTERY
THE PET SHOP MYSTERY
THE MYSTERY OF THE SECRET MESSAGE
THE FIREHOUSE MYSTERY
THE MYSTERY IN SAN FRANCISCO
THE NIAGARA FALLS MYSTERY
THE MYSTERY AT THE ALAMO
THE OUTER SPACE MYSTERY
THE SOCCER MYSTERY
THE MYSTERY IN THE OLD ATTIC
THE GROWLING BEAR MYSTERY
THE MYSTERY OF THE LAKE MONSTER
THE MYSTERY AT PEACOCK HALL
THE WINDY CITY MYSTERY
THE BLACK PEARL MYSTERY
THE CEREAL BOX MYSTERY
THE PANTHER MYSTERY
THE MYSTERY OF THE QUEEN'S JEWELS
THE STOLEN SWORD MYSTERY
THE BASKETBALL MYSTERY
THE MOVIE STAR MYSTERY
THE MYSTERY OF THE PIRATE'S MAP
THE GHOST TOWN MYSTERY
THE MYSTERY OF THE BLACK RAVEN
THE MYSTERY IN THE MALL
THE MYSTERY IN NEW YORK
THE GYMNASTICS MYSTERY
THE POISON FROG MYSTERY
THE MYSTERY OF THE EMPTY SAFE
THE HOME RUN MYSTERY
THE GREAT BICYCLE RACE MYSTERY

The Boxcar Children 20-Book Set includes Gertrude
Chandler Warner's original nineteen books,
plus an all-new activity book, stickers,
and a magnifying glass!

978-0-8075-0847-3 · US $132.81

978-0-8075-0925-8 · US $34.99

This fully illustrated edition
celebrates Gertrude Chandler
Warner's timeless story. Featuring
all-new full-color artwork as well as
an afterword about the author, the
history of the book, and the Boxcar
Children legacy, this volume will be
treasured by first-time readers
and longtime fans alike.

THE BOXCAR CHILDREN

GREAT ADVENTURE

An Exciting 5-Book Miniseries

Henry, Jessie, Violet, and Benny Alden are on a secret mission that takes them around the world!

When Violet finds a turtle statue that nobody's seen before in an old trunk at home, the children are on the case! The clue turns out to be an invitation to the Reddimus Society, a secret guild dedicated to returning lost treasures to where they belong.

Now the Aldens must take the statue and six mysterious boxes across the country to deliver them safely—and keep them out of the hands of the Reddimus Society's enemies. It's just the beginning of the Boxcar Children's most amazing adventure yet!

HC 978-0-8075-0695-0
PB 978-0-8075-0696-7

HC 978-0-8075-0698-1
PB 978-0-8075-0699-8

HC 978-0-8075-0684-4
PB 978-0-8075-0685-1

HC 978-0-8075-0687-5
PB 978-0-8075-0688-2

HC 978-0-8075-0681-3
PB 978-0-8075-0682-0

Also available as a boxed set!
978-0-8075-0693-6 · $34.95

Hardcover US $12.99 · Paperback US $6.99

HC 978-0-8075-0757-5 · US $12.99
PB 978-0-8075-0758-2 · US $6.99

Introducing The Boxcar Children Early Readers!

Adapted from the beloved chapter books, these new early readers allow kids to begin reading with the stories that started it all.

HC 978-0-8075-0839-8 · US $12.99
PB 978-0-8075-0835-0 · US $3.99

HC 978-0-8075-7675-5 · US $12.99
PB 978-0-8075-7679-3 · US $3.99

HC 978-0-8075-9367-7 · US $12.99
PB 978-0-8075-9370-7 · US $3.99

HC 978-0-8075-5402-9 · US $12.99
PB 978-0-8075-5435-7 · US $3.99

Check out other Boxcar Children Interactive Mysteries!

Strange things are happening at the grand reopening of the Gardner Hotel. Some people are saying the old building is haunted. Can you help the Aldens figure out what's really going on before the clock strikes midnight?

Look for the animated movie, *Surprise Island*!

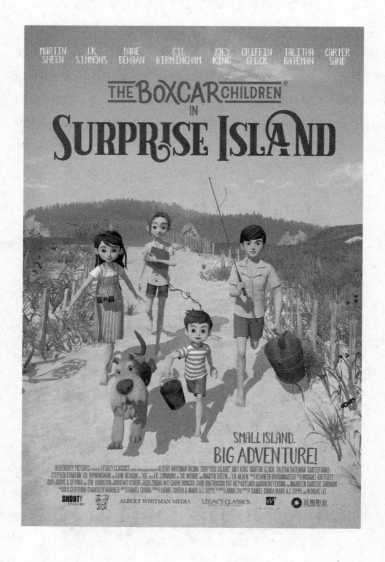

GERTRUDE CHANDLER WARNER discovered when she was teaching that many readers who like an exciting story could find no books that were both easy and fun to read. She decided to try to meet this need, and her first book, *The Boxcar Children*, quickly proved she had succeeded.

Miss Warner drew on her own experiences to write the mystery. As a child she spent hours watching trains go by on the tracks opposite her family home. She often dreamed about what it would be like to set up housekeeping in a caboose or freight car—the situation the Alden children find themselves in.

While the mystery element is central to each of Miss Warner's books, she never thought of them as strictly juvenile mysteries. She liked to stress the Aldens' independence and resourcefulness and their solid New England devotion to using up and making do. The Aldens go about most of their adventures with as little adult supervision as possible—something else that delights young readers.

Miss Warner lived in Putnam, Connecticut, until her death in 1979. During her lifetime, she received hundreds of letters from girls and boys telling her how much they liked her books.

NEW!
The Boxcar Children
DVD and Book Set!

This set includes Gertrude Chandler Warner's classic chapter book in paperback as well as the animated movie adaptation featuring Martin Sheen, J.K. Simmons, Joey King, Jadon Sand, Mackenzie Foy, and Zachary Gordon.

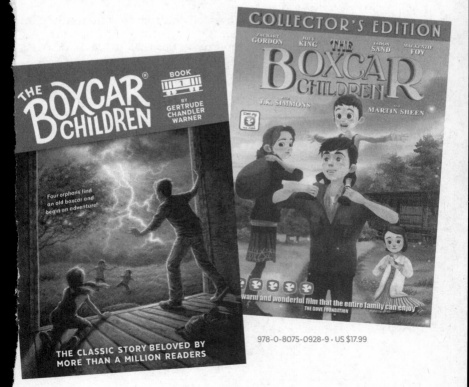